"We still can't decide whether she's more a Hillary or an Allison."

CONVERSATION HEARTS

John Crowley

Subterranean Press • 2008

First Edition

ISBN
978-1-59606-198-9

Subterranean Press
PO Box 190106
Burton, MI 48519

www.subterraneanpress.com

ON THE DAY BEFORE Valentine's Day the snow advancing from the west suddenly became a storm; the snow would cover them and then deepen rapidly (the radio weather said) toward the east as evening came. Perry and Lily (she in first, he in third grade) were sent home early from school, the telephone tree reaching the Nutting's house just as John Nutting was about to pick up the phone to call the Astra Literary Agency in Boston, to tell his wife that she should probably start for home as soon as she could. When he got the office, he was told that Ann-Marie, his wife's agent, was actually meeting Meg in a restaurant in Brookline. John considered calling the restaurant and paging her, but that seemed somehow too alarmist, and he sat and waited instead for the kids to get home.

The snow was already a couple of inches deep by the time the bus stopped in front of the house, so John lifted Lily off and carried her. Perry followed after with Lily's crutches. John set Lily down in the hall and helped with her coat.

"Now we can make valentines," Lily said, who had wanted to the night before, but John had got out the box of lace doilies and red hearts and glue and stickers too late, and Meg had said no, time for bed, causing something of an uproar for which John felt himself still in the doghouse all around. So now he said Yes they'd make valentines, and Perry sagged and groaned in a fine display of weary disgust, though John knew he actually liked making paper things of any kind and was (John thought) actually highly gifted, in a way; and all talking and thinking and disputing, they went into the kitchen and got going.

"Are you going to make valentines, Daddy?"

"I'm going to make one. For Mom."

"Is she your valentine?"

"I think so."

"Me too?"

"You too."

"Did Mom go to see Anne-Marie?" Perry asked.

"Yes, that's why she went. She wants to talk about her new book. The kid's book."

"Is it a chapter book?" Lily asked.

"Yes." John considered. "As I remember, it is a chapter book."

"I could read it," Perry said, with an air of negligent competence.

"I'm sure you could."

"What's the story about?" Lily asked. She actually knew, but liked to hear it again.

"It's about," John said, "a little girl who has no fur."

Lily laughed. "Girls don't have fur."

"You don't have fur?"

"No, Daddy."

"Well then maybe this book's about you."

"I doubt it," she said, grinning, which made Perry laugh aloud.

FIRST CHAPTER

When you look up into the sky at night, all the stars you can see are really suns, like the sun that shines on Earth. Some stars are bigger suns than our sun, and some are smaller; some are hotter, and some are not as hot. Some stars have planets going around them, just as Earth goes around our sun.

Maybe one star you can see on a clear dark night has a planet going around it that is like Earth, only different.

Maybe there are animals and people living on this planet who are like the people who live on Earth—only different.

Say the people are like us, and have hands and feet and two eyes (one eye on each side of their nose) and a mouth underneath; and two ears, one for each side of their heads. And heads too.

Only say that instead of plain skin they have beautiful thick soft fur all over, from head to foot, even on the backs of their hands and the tops of their feet.

And say that the bottoms of their feet are thick and tough as shoe-soles.

And say that the name of this planet is Brxx.

A woman named Qxx and a man named Fxx lay awake late at night in their house on the planet Brxx. It was a cold night, but the windows of their house were open. Actually the house didn't have any windows, only big open spaces in the walls through which the wind came in. Qxx and Fxx didn't mind, because they were both covered from head to foot in their own beautiful thick soft fur. Qxx's fur was red.

Qxx and Fxx were awake because they were thinking about the new baby that Qxx was soon to have. They were also awake because Qxx was so big with the new baby that she couldn't get comfortable in bed.

(Actually they didn't have a bed; they slept together on a wide flat rock, but they didn't mind because their thick fur was as good as a mattress and a blanket together.)

Since they couldn't sleep, they were talking about what they would name the new baby.

"I've always liked the name Trxx," said Qxx.

"I've always liked that name too," said Fxx. "But it's a girl's name. What if this baby is another boy?"

Qxx and Fxx already had a baby boy, named Pxx, who was curled up cozy and asleep in his own room, on the stone floor.

"It's not a boy," said Qxx. "I know."

"How do you know?" asked Fxx.

"I know," said Qxx.

✳ ✳ ✳

The new baby was a girl. But as soon as Fxx and Qxx saw her, they knew she was different from other babies.

Trxx was pink and smooth. Her eight tiny fingers were pink and her eight tiny toes were pink too. Her knees were wrinkled and so were her elbows. On top of her head there were a few strands of dark hair—but except for those, Trxx was naked all over.

Trxx had no fur.

"Oh dear," said Fxx. "Oh my stars."

"Oh," said Qxx. "Oh my baby." She was almost afraid to hold the newborn baby, she looked so strange.

"I'm sorry," said the doctor who had helped Trxx get born, whose name was Nxx. "It happens sometimes. Not very often. But it can happen. I'm so sorry," she said again, and she really was sorry.

Trxx didn't look like her brother Pxx when he was born; when Pxx was born he already had thick fur, over all his body, and on his feet he already had the beginnings of the thick tough pads that would protect his feet when he grew up and learned to walk. So did all the other babies born in the town that day, just as they had thick warm fur, red or brown or blue.

But Trxx didn't.

She didn't look like a baby of the planet Brxx at all. She looked a lot more like a baby of planet Earth. She looked like you and I looked when we were first born.

"Will she ever change?" asked Qxx. Her eyes filled with tears. "Will she ever grow fur and be like other people?"

"No," said Dr. Nxx, and her eyes filled with tears too. "No, she never will."

"Oh, my poor baby," Qxx. She started to cry.

Fxx started to cry too. So did little Pxx.

The only one who didn't cry was baby Trxx.

"All right," said Fxx, and he wiped his eyes with the fur of his hands. "All right, no more crying for a while.

"Not having fur is too bad. It's a bad deal, and it's going to be a lot of trouble for us, and a lot of trouble for Trxx. But she's our baby. And we love her."

"Just the way she is," said her brother Pxx.

"Yes," said her mother Qxx. "Just the way she is. And that's what matters most."

✳ ✳ ✳

"LOOK, DAD," Perry said. "Lily's jumping for joy."

Lily had recently figured out how to lift her whole body up off the floor with her crutches, like someone on a pogo stick; she lifted, dropped, lifted, dropped, in delight. Meg called it Jumping for Joy. Lily called it dancing. Sometimes she could turn herself around as she came down, so that she could actually jump in circles. She stopped after a while—it was surely pretty exhausting—and came to study what her father was doing.

"Is that the pin for Mom?" she said. He took it from its little box, out from its white blankets of cotton batting.

"Yes. Do you like it?"

Lily shrugged elaborately, who am I to say, but with a smirk of delight, in herself or the gesture or the day or the gift. The pin was dark steel, a pin for a coat lapel say, that was an arrow, made in such a way as to look when it was worn as though it pierced the fabric through, though it didn't really, it was an illusion; and on the arrow's top instead of an arrowhead was a hand, open, with a little garnet heart held in it.

"How are you going to wrap it? Is it going to be a surprise? Will she be surprised?"

"She's going to be so surprised."

"Do you know how to wrap it, Daddy?"

"Sure he knows," said Perry.

"Sure," John said, "I've got a plan. I can see it all."

It was John Nutting's strength and his weakness, as he had come to know: that seeing a thing as it might be or as he wanted it to be was to him what *having a plan* meant; that thought and care lavished on the picture of the thing that would come to be was the refining of the plan. What he'd thought of now, what he saw, was a heart, a full heart, a swollen heart, that could be opened and spill its contents—*what he had in his heart* was his idea. He had found a padded envelope of the kind you put fragile or special things in, that had a red stripe or tab or thread that the addressee was to pull to open. He wanted to somehow cut a heart shape out of this package in such a way that the pull-to-open stripe would run right down the center of the heart.

"Then see, Mom pulls the string thing, and the stuff inside comes out."

They looked at the parts of the project, what he had to put in, not themselves sure about this idea.

"You'll see," John said.

Inside the heart shape, before he sealed its edges with red tape (the dull brown color of the package was the downer part of the idea, but he couldn't see painting or coloring it), he was going to put a handful of candy hearts Along with these there was a long narrow strip of paper, folded accordion style, on which he had written these words:

Come on and TAKE A
Take another little piece of my heart, now, baby—
You know you got it, if it makes you feel good

So what he hoped, or saw, was that when the package was opened the little hearts would spill out, and the long folded strip spring forth a little to be taken hold of and pulled out and read, and the steel pin with the garnet heart appear last shyly among all this show. She'd laugh and she'd see and know. The little hearts were the pastel candy kind with little remarks printed on them in pink. He told the kids that they were called *conversation hearts*.

"Oh you kid," Perry read, from a blue one.

"They're candy, right?" asked Lily.

"Well sort of," John said. "I don't really know how good they are. I don't remember them being so hot. Not the point, in a way." Raggedy Ann and Andy had each had, under their rags and hidden within their stuffing, a conversation heart. It said *I love you* (as he remembered) and it was what animated them, brother and sister, made them live and talk. His own sister's Raggedy Ann doll was asserted to have one, but there was no way to be certain except to rip open her bosom and find it: his suggestion as to this was rejected.

"Cutie pie," read Perry. "Go girl. Get real."

He held that one out to Lily, who leaned forward, eyes closed and tongue out like a communicant, that same pious expectation too, and Perry put the heart on her tongue. He and John waited for her reaction. She let it melt, small smile on her face, then crushed it with open mouth. John then remembered the chalky tasteless sweetness.

"Be mine," Perry said. "New you. Howzat? Page me." He put on his Puzzlement face at that one, a comical screw.

"It means call me," John said. "Don't eat them all."

"Why not," said Perry, but this was another heart's message. He didn't seem tempted by them. His sister's reaction had not been enthusiastic. He often used her to test new edibles.

They'd thought, John and Meg, of getting a car phone: enough emergencies were now possible that it might be justified. Thinking, though, was all they'd done so far. Outside it was now all dark, and the falling snow was mounting without his monitoring its depth and intensity, which seemed to lessen his control of it, which was nil, then and now. If Meg left the meeting at five, she should be home by seven.

"Home soon," Perry said, and showed his father the yellow heart that said so.

NEXT CHAPTER

So Trxx went home with her mother and father and brother, wrapped in a soft blanket Dr. Nxx gave her.

She ate and slept and cried and made noises. She grew a little every day, and every day she saw new things and touched new things and heard new things. Everything in the world was new to Trxx, including Trxx herself.

She found out she had fingers and toes and learned to wiggle them. Soon she learned to smile and laugh. She laughed when her brother Pxx made faces at her, and when her mother tickled her, and when her father tossed her in the air and caught her.

She loved her mother and father and brother, and they loved her too, just the way she was. The hair on her head grew thicker and longer, but she never grew fur. She stayed just as she was when she was born.

Her mother and father learned to wrap Trxx up carefully in her warm blanket, and when it was cold at night they put her in between them on their bed to keep her warm. But when she learned to crawl she'd get out of her blanket and out from between her sleeping parents, and cry from the cold.

"If only we could figure out a way to keep this 'blanket' stuck on her, like fur," said Fxx.

They asked Dr. Nxx what to do. "What she needs is 'clothes,'" said Dr. Nxx.

"'Clothes?'" said Fxx and Qxx together.

"'Clothes' are like a blanket that fits over you and won't come off. All over. Nice and warm."

"All over?" said Qxx. "What about going to the bathroom?"

"Then you take them off."

"Every time?" said Qxx.

"Not all of them," the doctor said. "Don't worry. It's not as hard as it seems. You'll get used to it."

"And where," Fxx asked," do we get these 'clothes?'"

"I'll give you a prescription," said Dr. Nxx.

✳ ✳ ✳

There was a shirt, and a pants, and booties, and a little warm hat, and a warmer shirt to go over it all. The clothes cost a lot of flappers (that's what they call dollars on the planet Brxx) but at least they didn't come off every time Trxx wiggled, and leave her cold.

"How do you like it?" Qxx asked her daughter. "How do you like these clothes?"

Trxx just smiled and giggled. Her mother had never seen a baby that looked like Trxx with her clothes on, and she didn't know whether to laugh or cry.

Trxx grew fast, and needed more clothes all the time. They got dirty and had to be cleaned. They ripped and split as Trxx got bigger. The buttons fell off and rolled away and got lost.

"You'll need more buttons," Dr. Nxx said. "And some of this 'thread' and a 'needle.' Then you can sew the buttons on again when they come off."

"Hm," said Fxx. He took the tiny needle in his big hands. He'd never seen anything so impossible. "And where do we…"

"I'll give you a prescription," said Dr. Nxx.

✳ ✳ ✳

Winter came, and the weather got warm and the sun shone brightly. (On the planet Brxx it's warm in the winter and cold in the summer.) At last Trxx didn't need to get wrapped up in her shirt and pants and her socks and her other shirt and her little warm hat every day. She could go out with nothing on.

On a hot winter day Trxx's mother took her to the park to play without her clothes in the sun.

"Nice?" asked her mother.

"Nice," said Trxx. It was her first word.

But the other people in the park didn't think it was so nice. Some of them looked at Trxx all naked and furless, and their mouths would curl up in a way that seemed to mean they thought seeing Trxx all naked was creepy, or sad, or too bad. Other kids stopped what they were doing and stared at her.

"Does it hurt?" one person asked Qxx.

"No," said Qxx. "It doesn't hurt."

"Is she sick?" another person asked.

"No," Qxx said. "She's not sick."

"What happened to her?"

"She was born this way," said Qxx. "She's fine."

Trxx didn't know what the people were saying, and when they stared at her she stared back at them, and smiled.

But her brother Pxx hated the questions people asked.

"Why can't they mind their own business?" he said.

"They're curious," said Qxx.

"Well they should butt out," Pxx said.

"Why don't you go play whackball with those boys?" said Qxx.

But Pxx didn't want to leave his sister. He was bored and wanted to do something else but he was afraid that if he left something bad would happen to Trxx, even though he couldn't imagine what it would be. He didn't like the way people looked at her, and he didn't want her to be different.

"I wish I could give her my fur," he said. "If I could, I would."

"Fine," said his mother. "Then we'd have to buy clothes for *you*."

And then she put her arm around her son's shoulder and hugged him hard.

"So HOW are the kids?" Anne-Marie asked. "I never asked." Meg would have liked to order a great gleaming bowl of scarlet wine like the one Anne-Marie now lifted and sampled; but Anne-Marie was going home by cab, and Meg had a couple of hours of driving between here and home. The snow had just begun to show itself as something more than a bother out the windows.

"The kids are good. No bad news."

Anne-Marie laughed a little. "The only person I know who'd answer that question that way."

"Well they're fine. They do the things. They knock you out. They... I don't know. They're like the weather."

Anne-Marie's eyes, which could be beautiful when wide, were somewhat reptilian when hooded in doubt, if doubt was what she felt as she regarded Meg.

"So you got a chance to read that kid's book thing," Meg asked.

"I did. I liked it. It was fascinating. You know I love your things."

Meg waited for more.

"I gave it to someone who knows this market," Anne-Marie said. "I got a report and I made some notes." She plunged into her bag and did some business with papers that seemed to have come from a phone pad. "Did you know they have people at publishers of children's books who analyze the vocabulary, to see if the words used match the intended age of the readers?"

"Well I can imagine."

"They do."

"So what did this person think?"

"Well there's problems. Of course she liked it and wanted you to know that."

Meg said nothing.

Anne-Marie glanced at her notes. "She says. It's too short for a chapter book but the words and sentences are too hard for an I-can-read-it-myself book, and the subject matter is too hard for a picture book."

"Really."

"Another thing," Anne-Marie said, putting the notes away. "In a kid's book, as she sees it and I believe this, you can't go switching the point of view too often. It's best to stick to one point of view, one kid or one animal or one grandma or whatever. I think you especially can't have parents' point of view overwhelming the child's point of view. I think that happens in this."

"I didn't realize there were so many rules," Meg said. "In fact actually I don't think there *are* so many. I know the books Perry and Lily love. There's not always…" She stopped then, though, because she saw she had come up on a crux that arises between writer and agent, or writer and publisher, or writer and reader finally: they see something wrong, something that fails, and they don't really know how to say what it is, something in the toils of the story, sometimes in its core, but what is it? They think they know, and they say "The plot's not involving" or "The characters aren't sympathetic" or "The point of view is wrong," which sound like objective errors being pinned down, but which, *a*, aren't that at all but only a way of saying I don't like it, and *b*, are therefore impossible to counter with reasonable arguments, and *c*, no good at all to you as the writer. The only thing worse than leaving it as it is, wounded and feeble, would be to try to fix it by the formulas they give you.

"Listen," Anne-Marie said. "I know how important this is to you. I know what you're trying to do with this, to write about the prejudice, the prejudice against people who are different. I get that, and I of course understand. But I just don't think it's going to fly in the children's book world. Something that's so, you know, directly instructional. They just shy away from stuff like that."

"Uh huh."

"I wonder if there's some way to get it out under the sponsorship of some group."

"Some group?"

"Well you know, a group that has an educational purpose. Like a group that deals with the problem this is addressing."

Meg could see the kind of book or booklet Anne-Marie meant. Such things were in every waiting room she went to with Lily, every office. "Okay," she said. "Never mind. It was just a thing. Thanks for checking it out."

"It's not going to go to waste," Anne-Marie said.

"No. I know. Look, Anne-Marie, I appreciate your trying."

Anne-Marie drank. "So to get back to your new Anna Wolfe story. They're very excited." She didn't communicate excitement. "But you know how it is. If they don't get involved they think they aren't important and don't really have a job."

"Okay." A weariness had begun to spread upward from her feet or her knees toward her heart and head. She wasn't tired of her girl detective, but she was getting tired of talking about her. Take it or leave it. She didn't have the clout, though.

"First there's what you want to call it—'Delphic Oracle'? Isn't that a little, I don't know, remote?"

"Well you know what the Delphic oracle was, right?"

"Darling, of course *I* know, but will your readers and bookbuyers know? What are you hoping they'll get from this title?"

"Well I thought it was good because of the ambiguity. Oracles are true but you don't know in what sense, until they've come true. They can be true and yet turn out not to mean at all what you thought they meant. And you have to beware of bringing into being the thing you first thought the oracle meant, usually by trying to avoid it."

"Like Oedipus."

"Right."

"So this relates how?"

Meg crossed her hands as in prayer and bent toward her agent, the only agent she'd ever had. "Well it's a little like Lily." Anne-Marie was one of the first to know about the ultrasound that showed Lily would have problems. It was just a routine scan, and done in Boston; she and Meg had planned on lunch after. "You get a diagnosis, and a prognosis. A prediction. A prophecy. Anyway an oracle. Ambiguous, like they all are."

"Okay," she said.

"Then at the far end, you look back and say Yes it was predicted to be this way. But it wasn't. Not necessarily; not all of it; not what it's *like*."

"So the oracle can bring about what it predicts. That's a responsibility. Because the oracle might be wrong."

"The oracle isn't wrong," Meg said. "It just isn't determining. What you hope is that you'll learn better as you go, learn that the possibilities are greater than they seemed. *You* determine. You and the gods. The Greeks knew."

"They knew everything." Anne-Marie lit a cigarette, this restaurant being one that let her, which is why she came here. "Except the book business."

Meg reached for the gloves that lay beside her plate. The sense of hopeless incapacity got a little higher: the book business, other people, the weather; the things her life had come to be about, the fight against prediction. "Anne-Marie, I've got to go. I'm getting scared. It's been coming down heavier ever since we got here."

"Weather man said only a couple of inches."

"Yeah?" Meg said. "That's what he predicted?"

They both laughed. "We'll do this," Anne-Marie said. "I feel it'll work out."

"Sure," Meg said. "What's that thing the Chinese say? Tell me again, Auntie Anne-Marie."

"The Chinese say," Anne-Marie said, her favorite catch-phrase, "'When we reach the mountain, the road upward will appear.'"

CHAPTER AFTER
THE ONE BEFORE

Trxx grew up. She learned to talk. She was angry sometimes and cried sometimes and sometimes she wanted everything in the world and she wanted it *right now* and really screamed. But most of the time she was happy. "As happy as the day is long," said Qxx.

"What does that mean?" Trxx asked her.

"I don't know what it means. But it's what you are. Now where's your shirt?"

"Shirt! I don't want to!"

"Here it is!" said her brother Pxx.

Pxx had learned to help his mother put on her clothes and take them off and even wash and dry them. But Trxx took a lot of time to get dressed, and changed; she couldn't run out of the house every morning like Pxx could, because she had to get dressed first.

And sometimes she didn't want to get dressed at all.

"Shirt!"

"I don't want to!" said Trxx, and started to run.

"Shirt!" said Pxx, and chased after her,

"Trxx!" said her mother, and chased after her too.

Imagine: Trxx was nearly six, and she was smart and handy, and she still couldn't put on her own clothes! But that was because she didn't know she was supposed to be able to, and neither did her mother or her father. Nobody said to her: "Oh, everybody who's six can put their own shirt on! Everybody who's six can tie their own shoes!"

Because nobody else could.

✳ ✳ ✳

Of course all the other kids in the neighborhood where Trxx grew up had thick fur, black or blue or red, and thick pads on the soles of their feet, just like her brother Pxx. Some were older than Trxx, and were mostly her brother's friends; and some were just her age.

Mostly the kids in the neighborhood liked Trxx and played with her and didn't think all the time that she was the Girl who Had No Fur.

But sometimes her friends talked to her as though she were a baby, and sometimes they treated her as though she were a doll or a pet. Sometimes they wanted to be best friends, and sometimes they told her to go away, because she couldn't play the same games as other people.

They weren't really being mean. They just forgot, sometimes, that—except for having no fur—Trxx was just like them.

"So are you going to go to school?" they asked her one cold day of summer, when everybody was thinking about school starting. All of Trxx's friends were going to be in the first grade.

"Sure," said Trxx.

"You are?"

"Sure. Why not?"

All of Trxx's friends stared at Trxx, and looked at each other as though they knew something she didn't know.

When Trxx came in from playing, she had a blister on her ankle.

"Trxx!" her mother said. "You have to wear a *sock* with your *shoe* or you get a blister. You know that!"

"Mom," Trxx said. "Am I really going to go to school?"

"You bet you are, my darling dear," her mother said. "You bet you are."

"But," Trxx said. "What if the teacher doesn't like people with no fur?"

"She does. You met her, Trxx. She likes you."

"What if the kids don't like people with no fur?"

"They'll like you. Some of them are your own friends, Trxx."

Her mom was trying to clean Trxx's heel and get a bandage on. It took her a long time, because she had only done it once before. *Your* mom does it very quickly, because she's put bandages on blisters ever since she was a little kid herself.

"What if my shoes come untied?" Trxx said. "Who will tie them?"

"I'll come to school at lunchtime," her mother said. "Just to check." She helped Trxx put on one shoe. "And pretty soon, Trxx, you'll be able to tie them yourself."

"I can't!"

"You'll learn. I learned. Watch."

Qxx tied Trxx's shoes again. While she tried to tie the lace, her tongue came out and curled up. Her furry fingers got stuck in the laces. You could have tied Trxx's shoes in a minute, but Trxx's mother took a long time.

✳ ✳ ✳

One day Qxx found about another child in town who had also been born with no fur.

"Is it a girl?" Trxx asked. "Like me?"

"No, a boy," said her mother. "His name is Jaxx."

"How old is he?" Trxx wanted to know. "Six, like me?"

"He's eight," said her mother. "But I think he's very nice."

Trxx and her mother got ready to go visit the boy with no fur. It was a cold day in summer, and they had to put on almost every piece of clothes Trxx had.

"Someday," said Qxx to her daughter, "you are going to have to learn to do all these things for yourself!" She was a little impatient and tugged and pulled Trxx's clothes on.

"I will," Trxx said. "Someday."

"*And* tie your shoes."

"I will," Trxx said. "Someday."

"Someday *soon*," said her mother.

Trxx watched her mother and thought: "I'll never learn."

But she would.

✳ ✳ ✳

The boy who had no fur lived on the other side of town, and Qxx and Trxx took the buxx to see him. On the buxx, a woman with bright orange fur kept staring at Trxx. Trxx stared back, and smiled. When Trxx smiled, she saw a little tear well up in the lady's eye.

"Brave little thing!" the woman said. "Brave little tyke, putting up with so much!"

"Oh good grief," Qxx said, so only Trxx could hear. She looked down at her daughter and rolled her eyes so only Trxx could see. Trxx laughed, because that was what her mother always did when people said that Trxx was brave. She said *Oh good grief* and rolled her eyes.

Trxx wondered why people thought she was brave to have no fur. She was brave when she climbed tall trees and brave when she went to sleep with no night light and brave when she got a shot without freaking out. But what was so brave about having no fur and having to wear clothes?

"I don't understand people sometimes, Mom," she said.

"Neither do I, darling," said her mother. "But then I think a lot of people don't understand us, either."

✳ ✳ ✳

Jaxx and his mother were glad to see Trxx and Qxx. *They* could understand one another just fine.

"Having no fur sort of runs in our family," Jaxx's mother said. She showed them a funny old picture. "My great-uncle Braxx had the same condition. He used to travel with a circus, along with the sword-swallower and the fire-eater. He was called 'Braxx the All-Bare, The Amazing Furless Man'. He had some clothes made that looked just like most people's fur. He would slowly pull them off, until he had nothing on. Just skin. Some people would faint."

"Wasn't he embarrassed?" Trxx asked. "With all those people looking at him?"

"Well, not after a while. He said he loved show business. And people did pay a flapper apiece to see him."

✳ ✳ ✳

While Qxx and Jaxx's mother sat in the kitchen and drank hot gurgle and talked about where to get clothes made cheap, Jaxx and Trxx played together.

They talked while they played, about everything in the world. About clothes and how awful they were. About what it would be like if it were hot in the summer and cold in the winter, instead of the other way around the way it is on the planet Brxx. They talked about getting sunburned (nobody else knew what that felt like) and going swimming naked (nobody else knew what that felt like, either.)

Jaxx called other people "the furballs" and made Trxx laugh.

"Jaxx," she said. "I have a question."

"What's the question?" said Jaxx.

"What do you say when a little kid or somebody comes up to you and stares at you and goes *What's the matter with you?*"

"That's easy," Jaxx said. "I tell them I'm from another planet." He stood up and stuck out his chest. "I tell them I came here to Brxx from another planet, and I tell them that on *my* planet *nobody* has fur and everybody looks like me. And that on my planet I have super-powers so they better watch out."

Trxx laughed. Trxx's mother laughed too, and Jaxx's mother smiled and shook her head.

"And," said Jaxx, "I tell them that if any *furballs* ever ended up on my planet, we'd probably put them in the *zoo*."

Trxx laughed so hard she almost fell down. She didn't think Jaxx really said that to people who asked him *What's wrong with you?* or *What happened to you?* But ever after, when somebody asked her a question like that, she would think of Jaxx, and laugh.

A WEEK or two after the ultrasound had shown them Lily wound palely inside Meg, her flawed spine traceable like the spine of a translucent guppy, a snow storm like this one had fallen over their house. It was one of those spring snowstorms that come down in big sodden flakes and layer the trees as though with thick pudding or wet wash, comical-seeming snow that's not funny in fact; it began in the night and when morning came and John went out to the porch it was grievous. The tall arbor-vitae cedars that stood in pairs on the corners of the lot were so heavy-headed that they had bent nearly double, and the low branches of the big firs in the back were laid down into the mounting heap as though consumed. As soon as the fall of it subsided, John pulled on boots and took a broom and a long-handled plastic rake and labored out through it to the cedars, to try to knock off enough snow to release them, so they wouldn't break; he beat at the branches and combed with the plastic rake, and some of the branches did lift away like arms freed from shackles, and the tree raised its head a little, but some of the branches, some of the biggest too and not the small springy ones, didn't snap free. Broken. One whole secondary trunk of the smaller of the pair, broken, unresponsive. When he had done all he could, throat seared with cold and boots filled with snow, he made his way to the firs, going down on his knees once as he waded forward. God damn it, he breathed. God damn it. It was so unfair, a snow so heavy, so wrong that spring could come so close and then do this. He reached the firs and it was the same: he beat at the bound limbs to knock away their burden and some lifted free and grateful, amazing resilience, flinging snow in his face as they went up, but some not, inert, unable to rise, broken, you couldn't see beneath the smothering snow which was hurt and which wasn't. He tugged at them with icy hands to pull them free, but some wouldn't come up when he had loosened them, couldn't spring.

He sat back at last exhausted. He was weeping in anger and hurt. God damn it, he said again and again. God damn New England. Cruel, cruel New England.

Perry and Lily had grown tired of valentines; they piled theirs in two piles and John hid away the valentine for Meg to put with her breakfast next day. Then he made popcorn for dinner, something Meg sometimes did on nights of emergency or hurry or many urgent claims, which this seemed somehow to be even though they couldn't do anything but sit. When a car came close and stopped—they could only see its lights and hear the slow milling of its tires out on the road—it turned out to be the newspaper deliverer, hero or dope out on his rounds in his ancient Chevy Malibu. Perry pulled on boots and coat and went out to the box at the driveway's end to get their paper, and then sat eating popcorn and turning big pages one by one, reading the headlines aloud, letting Lily and John know the news. The high school was putting on *A Midsummer Night's Dream* and there were to be real flying fairies in it.

"It's a play by Shakespeare," John said. "There are fairies in it."

"Real flying fairies?"

"Well actually it says with wires," John said, looking over Perry's shoulder.

Perry studied the text, brows knit with effort to decode the false claims. Kids from middle school were being recruited to be Peaseblossom and Cobweb. Flying. Perry wondered if he envied them.

"Usually the fairies don't fly in this play," John said. "They just well sort of trip."

"They *trip*?" asked Lily. That smile of wonder she had at things, at things she didn't get, as though they tickled her by their weirdness. Always. When she'd started to talk her first complete sentence was *Where'd come from*? About some object that she hadn't suspected would be produced before her, what was it, a bar of Castile soap, a rubber duck, a bunch of flowers. *Where'd come from*? In delight and confusion.

"I mean they sort of dance along. Tripping." He did some tripping, little steps, winglike arms fluttering delicately. "Where the bee sucks, there suck I," he sang in falsetto. "In the cowslip's bell I lie."

Perry danced too, flying; then pretended to trip and fall, flail to stay upright, trip again, regain balance. Lily jumped and spun. The phone rang and stilled them.

"How is it there?" Meg asked.

"It's not good. They're saying six to eight inches. But you know how it is. Every county's different. It could be okay all the way till you start up the hills."

"Well I'm coming," Meg said. "We're done here."

"How did it go?"

"I'll explain," she said. "What are you guys doing?"

"Tripping," said John.

NEXT-TO-LAST CHAPTER

Every weekmiddle, Fxx, Trxx's father, went to play whackball with his friends. (On the planet Brxx, they don't have weekends, but they do take two days off in the middle of the week, and that's called the weekmiddle.)

Fxx was an excellent whackball player, and over time he had practiced and got better and better. Almost every time he played, he beat his friends easily.

One weekmiddle day after they had finished a game and Fxx had won again, he said with a grin: "Well, this isn't much fun."

His friends agreed. They decided the only way to make the game fun again was to give Fxx a *handicap*. That means they made it harder for Fxx to play, so that the game would be more even. What they did was to make Fxx tie one hand behind his back.

With the handicap, one hand tied behind his back, Fxx had to try much harder. He had to think carefully at every stroke. His friends got way ahead at first, and though Fxx did well, considering his handicap, one of his friends won that game.

As they were all laughing together at the end of the game, Fxx suddenly had a thought:

"This must be what it's like for Trxx," he thought. "Trxx is playing with a handicap. She's just like everybody else, but with something taken away. Like my hand tied behind my back."

When he came home that night he told Qxx what he had thought of. "Trxx is playing with a handicap," he said. "She's just like everybody else, but with something missing."

"Hmm," said Qxx.

"That means she has to try harder, but if she does, she can do anything she wants."

"Hmm," said Qxx. "I don't know. I have to think about that." She didn't like thinking that Trxx was like everybody else, except with something missing. But maybe Fxx was right.

✳ ✳ ✳

That night Qxx dreamed that there really was a planet like the one Jaxx pretended he came from. She dreamed she went there in a spaceship.

On this planet everyone was like Trxx and Jaxx: they had no fur at all, only a little hair on the tops of their heads or on their faces. All of them, every one, had to wear clothes all the time, and shoes too.

She saw them, in her dream, going up and down the streets, in and out of the stores and houses, every one of them in their clothes: shoes and socks and pants and coats and hats and scarfs and mittens.

Some of the stores they went in sold nothing but clothes. Of course! If everyone needed them, they would be for sale everywhere! No wondering where to get them, no prescription from the doctor! Store after store with clothes for men and women, little clothes for boys and girls, whole stores with nothing but tiny clothes for babies! Qxx almost cried in her dream to see them.

In their houses, these people had special little rooms to put all their different clothes in, and special hangers to hang them on. They had long mirrors in their bedrooms to look at themselves in and see if their clothes were straight and neat. People didn't have just one set of clothes or two sets, they had many different sets, dozens of different shirts and socks and scarves and hats. They had clothes to go swimming in. They had clothes to go to bed in.

They even had clothes for their beds!

And the most amazing thing of all was that nobody thought that wearing clothes was strange.

Qxx laughed in her dream as she sailed over this amazing impossible planet. She thought: If nobody has fur, then not having fur is normal.

The people of this planet didn't think it was brave to wear clothes; they didn't think it was dreadful, and they didn't think it was special. They didn't mind wearing them, or buying them, or keeping them clean. No little tear welled up in people's eyes when they saw children in their funny clothes; nobody made the creepy mouth to see other people without their clothes on and their bare skin showing; nobody made fun of them, either.

Wearing clothes was normal.

Qxx dreamed that she landed her spaceship and stepped out. And in her dream, Qxx saw the people of the planet turn to look at her. And she looked down at herself to see the bright red fur that clothed her from head to foot.

Qxx understood, just then, how Trxx felt when people stared at her, and tried to figure her out. It was very uncomfortable.

The people of the planet in their clothes and hats and shoes came closer, with expressions of amazement and even fear on their bare faces. Qxx thought some of them might faint, as the people did who came to see Braxx the All-Bare.

"Hey," said Qxx. She held out her arms to show herself, furry as could be. "Hey! It's normal for me!"

Then she woke up.

✳ ✳ ✳

THIS PREJUDICE against people who are different. Meg pondered that, Anne-Marie's summary of what her probably foolish little book had been about, and wondered how she'd got that idea. Was there something in it that would push a reader toward that, or was it just what the reader expected to see there and so saw it anyway? Anne-Marie was probably right that it wasn't really a children's book at all, only sort of seemed like one, but what it was *about* ought to have been clear. If everybody could fly (Meg explained to no one) then anyone who couldn't would be at a disadvantage: even though they'd be just as able as they are now. Because everything would be arranged for people who could fly. That's all. "That's all," she said aloud, and just then realized she had been carelessly turning out of her lane into a less-plowed one to pass a truck. She felt her heart in her mouth (one of those phrases that make no sense until you've felt it) and fell back with care into the safer lane, her wipers wiping furiously at the snow flung up by the truck.

Pay attention, she said within. I'll pay attention.

It was a long time, but she was now in sight of what she thought of as the half-way mark, the stacks of a chemical plant of some kind, lit luridly, hard to apprehend from a distance, its floodlit smoke rising into the blowing snow, like a Turner storm done in black and white. Half way. But now along the road she began to see cars on the margins, in the breakdown lane, sometimes askew or otherwise seeming not to be there on purpose; sometimes a dome-light on, shining within a car rapidly coming to be covered with snow, a lamp lit in an igloo. It was bad. It was evidently and obviously really not good.

She began to think that it was stupid, she'd been stupid, should have stayed over, found a hotel, she was almost beginning to think she should pull off now into the streets of Sturbridge or Brimfield and find a motel: she could envision the streets she would have to get through, the quick-falling snow veiling the streetlights, the local plows maybe not out, no it was hopeless: she told herself so, told herself it wasn't the way you do this, considering hopeless alternatives, visualizing hopeless escapes. You just keep on: you keep on and cover every mile, one at a time, not in advance or in hope but only by doing it, and only counting it as done when it was done. Just keep on, she thought. Just keep on steady.

John thought of her thinking these things, envisioned her seeing these things, both the cars she saw along the highway margins and the streets and roads of villages that she pictured; he thought of her going on, telling herself how to go on. So often had they both traveled that stretch of Interstate, going to or from things that had been hard or impossible to imagine in advance or carrying home consequences that couldn't be calculated: operations and consultations and examinations. Prognoses. He could see her, the seat snugged up tightly to the steering wheel the way she liked it, both her hands at the top of the wheel and her head slightly forward, as though to see a little farther into what was coming.

LAST CHAPTER

When Qxx woke up she remembered: today is the first day of school.

"Mom!" Trxx called. "Help!"

Qxx jumped up. Outside the cold wind blew and the rain fell. It was a cold summer day. Trxx was trying to get her shirt on, and her head was stuck in the head hole, and her left arm was stuck in the right arm hole.

She was learning to put on her own clothes, but sometimes she got confused.

Trxx was up especially early, because her mother knew it would take her longer than most kids to get ready for school. After all, if you're covered with thick fur, and you don't wear jammies and you don't wear clothes, all you have to do is get up, eat your crackles and drink your slurp, brush your teeth and go. You don't even have to make your bed!

But Trxx took longer. Even when everybody helped.

"Shoes," said Fxx. "On."

"No no," said Qxx. "Socks first, remember?"

"Ah," said Fxx. "Socks."

"Pants," said Pxx.

"No no," said Trxx. "Underpants first!"

"Oh yeah," said Pxx.

"Mittens!" Qxx said to Trxx. "Hat!"

When Trxx was all ready, and her hair was brushed (and Pxx's fur was brushed) and her hat was tied on and her scarf was knotted around her neck, the others stood for a minute and looked at her.

"Hey," said Fxx. "First grader!"

Trxx was all ready to go when she decided to have one more bite of crackles and one more sip of slurp to give her strength. But when she picked up her big cup in her mitten hand, it slipped. It started to slip and kept on slipping faster while everybody stared in horror and couldn't move.

Then Pxx jumped and tried to catch the cup. Too late!

"Oh no! Trxx!"

"Oops," said Trxx. "Oh no."

Trxx was covered from scarf to shoes with sticky brown slurp. Ugh!

Her coat was wet, and so they took that off. Underneath, her shirt was wet, so they took that off too, and her pants. Underneath her pants her underpants were wet, so they took them off.

The stuff had even got into her shoes. Her socks were wet, and she had to take them off too.

Then they had to start all over again.

"I can't do this," Trxx moaned. "I'll never be able to."

"You can do anything you want," said Qxx. "You can do what you want to do. It just takes you a little longer."

"A lot longer," Trxx said angrily.

"Sometimes a lot longer," said Qxx.

"Like hours."

"Then we'll get up earlier," said Qxx.

"Then I'll be tired."

"We'll go to sleep earlier."

"Oop, there they go," said Pxx.

He pointed out the window.

Across the field the other kids were

running and tumbling and yelling and chasing after each other on their way to school. The wind howled and the cold rain fell, but the kids laughed at it. In school they would sit in their seats in their warm coats and the smell of drying fur would fill the room.

Trxx looked after them. They were getting farther and farther away. She was going to be last.

Of course.

For a minute, just for a minute, Trxx decided that she would never put on her stupid clothes ever again, and never go outside again, just stay inside and cover herself up with her mother and father the way she had when she was a baby, and sleep forever.

That made her sad.

And then she got mad.

Suddenly she jumped up. "Okay!" she said. "Underpants!"

"Underpants," Qxx said. "Right." She found underpants.

"Socks!" Trxx shouted. "One for each foot!" She struggled into her underpants while her parents and Pxx looked for her only other pair of socks.

Fxx brought the socks. Trxx pulled them on.

"Shoes!" Trxx shouted, like a general in a war. "Shirt! Pants! Coat!"

Pxx and Fxx found a sort-of clean shirt and the shoes and her old pants. Trxx pulled her shoes on.

Then she tied them.

"Trxx!" said her mother. "You tied your shoes!"

Everybody looked down at Trxx's shoes.

"You did it," said Pxx. "Wow."

Trxx looked down at her shoes too, and they seemed a little bit farther away than they had been the day before. Maybe she was getting taller.

"You did it," said her father.

"Sure," she said. "Mom, I'm late!"

She grabbed her bag and Pxx grabbed his bag and they ran out (they didn't need to open the door, because there wasn't any door) and ran across the field.

Qxx and Fxx stood in the doorway waving to their children.

"I forgot to get a kiss," said Fxx. "Shucks."

Qxx saw Trxx stop and bend down to tie her shoe again. When she bent over her hat fell off. She picked it up and jammed it on her head, and then ran after Pxx.

Qxx thought of the dream she had dreamed, where everyone in the world had no fur, and wore clothes.

If *everybody* had to get dressed every morning, Trxx wouldn't be last: not every time. Somebody else would forget their socks or their hat or forget how to tie their shoes.

"Tough job," said Fxx.

"You're wrong," Qxx said.

"It's not a tough job?"

"I mean what you said yesterday. About Trxx."

"Oh?"

"It's not true."

"What did I say?" Fxx asked

Fxx had said that Trxx was the same as everyone else, except that she had a *handicap*—something taken away or held back from her, something normal people had but she didn't have, something she had to get along without.

But that wasn't true.

Trxx *wasn't* the same as everyone else.

No one is the same as everyone else.

Trxx was Trxx, and the way Trxx was, was normal for Trxx.

"Life isn't whackball," she said to Fxx.

Fxx looked surprised. "I never said it was," he said.

"Well don't forget it," said Qxx. "Trxx isn't a normal person with something missing. Trxx is Trxx. She's being all she can be, and that's as much as you or me or Pxx or anyone on this planet can be."

Qxx put her furry arm through Fxx's furry arm. She watched her daughter as she ran out of sight.

"It's all that anyone can be," she said. "On any planet anywhere."

✳ ✳ ✳

"*THERE* SHE is," said John. "There she is."

"There she is," the kids said, who had never doubted she would come, did not yet need to wonder whether she might not. Silently she'd entered the driveway, the car's sound swallowed with all other sound by the snow, but the searching lights sweeping over the dark lawn as she turned in to the driveway and then illuminating the closed door of the garage—they could see the light from the kitchen, sign of homecoming. Once, you left a light burning for the returning one; now the returning one's own lights brought her home, announced her arrival.

O You Kid. I Love You. Way to Go. What A Babe. Love Life. Page Me. U R Mine. Lily and Perry followed him to the door out to the garage, welcoming committee; Lily watched her father and Perry go to pull up the door, watched the car creep forward through the drift by now as high as the bumpers, chewing the snow as it came forward, coming breathing hotly into the bright space.

"Hi, hi."

"God, some night."

"Yes. We were worried."

"I'm all right," Meg said, climbing out. The car's underparts were thick with clotted snow like a wintering buffalo's.

"Did Anne-Marie like your book?" Perry asked.

"Not much," Meg said.

"Uh oh," Perry said.

Of course she was all right. She was all right all along, or at least now it was evident that all along she had been all right. John Nutting felt a spasm of recapitulatory relief of a kind he was becoming familiar with, though he hadn't known it in his life, or at least he hadn't noticed it, until the day Lily first got out of the hospital.

"Mom!" Lily cried to her from the door. "Come see what we made! Dad made a heart! We made valentines!"

"I'm coming, hon, I'm coming."

It had also been snowing on that day when Lily had first of got out of the hospital where she'd been born, only a few flakes though blown around out of an iron sky, almost too cold for snow. Lily was nearly a month old and had yet to see outdoors, yet to be outside. Meg had gone to the parking garage to get the car and told John to bring Lily out to the curb and watch for it. So it was he who took her out. He lifted her from the hospital bassinet at the exit door and wrapped her in her own blanket, bought for her by her grandmother before she was born, hope against hope, and he tugged her hat down; made her a papoose inside the blanket, pressed her to him, and (tugging down his own hat) he just walked out into the day, a con walking free after having finished his sentence, or con-man having pulled off his scam. Don't look back. Lucky, he'd felt so damn lucky, knew they were all lucky, though what he and she and Meg from now on would mean by "lucky" might not be what everyone else meant. They weren't the same as everyone else: no one is. *You're out* he'd said in exalted wonderment to her small face. *You got out, Lily. You got out.* And of course she had, because here she now was, Jumping for Joy as her mother came into the house on a gust of cold air. That's how it is, how it would be, for them all: when they had come through all right, it would be seen that, of course, all along they must have: all along.